First American Edition.
Copyright © 1980 by The Walt Disney Company.
All rights reserved under International and Pan-American Copyright
Conventions. Published in the United States by Random House, Inc.,
New York, and simultaneously in Canada by Random House of Canada
Limited, Toronto. Originally published in Denmark as LILLE ULV I
SKURKELAERE by Gutenberghus Bladene, Copenhagen.
ISBN: 0-394-84625-7 (trade); 0-394-94625-1 (lib. bdg.)
Manufactured in the United States of America
90   C D E F G H I J K

WALT DISNEY PRODUCTIONS
presents

The Big Bad Wolf and Li'l Wolf

Random House 🏠 New York

Li'l Wolf ran home from school.
He was so happy.
He had won a gold star!

"Dad, look at the star I won!" he said.
"It is for being good!"

"Good?" said his father. "I am the *Big
Bad Wolf*. I give people trouble! You are
supposed to do that, too."

"Gee, Dad, I do not want you to be
unhappy," said Li'l Wolf.

"Oh, but I am," the Big Bad Wolf groaned.

"I know," the Big Bad Wolf said.
"Tomorrow I will teach you how
to be bad!"

Li'l Wolf wanted to please his father.

"Dad," he said, "I was going to go on a
picnic with the Three Little Pigs tomorrow.
But I'd rather go out with you."

Then he served his father a tasty dinner.

Li'l Wolf washed the dishes.

And the Big Bad Wolf thought about the bad things he could teach Li'l Wolf.

Hmm, he thought. We can steal the picnic lunch away from the Three Little Pigs.

That will be a good lesson in being bad.

The next day father and son went to the woods.
The Big Bad Wolf found a path in the woods.
I cannot wait to steal the Three Little Pigs' lunch,
thought the Big Bad Wolf.

"Li'l Wolf, here's the first lesson," said
the Big Bad Wolf. "Go down this path to the
restaurant. When no one is looking, throw a
rock through the restaurant's window.
That's mischief lesson number one."

"Then call the police. Tell them that the Three Little Pigs threw the rock. That's mischief lesson number two!"

"Gosh, Dad, they are my friends," said
Li'l Wolf.

But Li'l Wolf knew he must obey
his father.
Off he went.

Li'l Wolf went
to the restaurant.
He picked up
a rock.
He looked at
the window.
But he just
could not do it.

He could not throw the
rock through the window.

Oh, dear, he thought.
What am I going to do?

Just then the Three Little Pigs walked by.
"Here you are, Li'l Wolf," said
Practical Pig. "We were afraid you might
miss the picnic."

"I still might," said Li'l Wolf sadly.
"My dad is teaching me how to be bad. I must
throw a rock through the window. Then I
have to say *you* did it. I do not want to do
that. But he wants to hear the glass crash!"

"What a problem!" said Practical Pig. "Let's all think about what we can do."

After a few minutes Practical Pig spoke. "I have an idea. I saw a big old tin pan under a tree. Come with me!"

"There is the pan," said Practical Pig.
"We'll throw stones into it. The noise will
sound like broken glass! We will fool that
Big Bad Wolf."

SMASH! CRASH!
Everyone in the woods heard the noise.

The Big Bad Wolf heard the crashes, too.

"He did it!" the Big Bad Wolf shouted.

CRASH!

"He did it again! He broke another window. I knew he could be bad!"

The Big Bad Wolf crept through the woods quickly.

"Now he will blame the Three Little Pigs for the broken windows!" He laughed to himself.

Meanwhile, Li'l Wolf and two of the little pigs were playing.

But Practical Pig said, "Wait a minute!

"The Big Bad Wolf will see that no windows are broken. Let's cover up some windows. We will use the towels on that line."

"That is a good idea," said Li'l Wolf.
They took three towels from the line.
Then they hung them across three
windows.

"There!" said Practical Pig. "Li'l Wolf,
your father will think you broke *three*
windows!"

"Great!" said Li'l Wolf. "But let's
leave before he gets here."
They ran into the woods.
But they forgot their picnic baskets.

At last the Big Bad Wolf got to the restaurant.

He was pleased to see three windows covered up.

He was even more pleased to find the picnic baskets.

"What a feast Li'l Wolf and I will have!" he said. "Now I must find him."

In the woods, Li'l Wolf and the Three
Little Pigs found an empty house.
"Let's go inside," said one little pig.
But the front door and windows were
nailed shut.

"Maybe the back door is open," said Li'l Wolf.
He ran around the house very fast.
He did not see the old well.
CRUNCH! SPLASH!!
Li'l Wolf tripped and fell into the well!

"Li'l Wolf! What happened?" the
Three Little Pigs cried.
They had heard the splash.

"Where are you?" they asked.
"In the well," called Li'l Wolf.
"There is not much water. But I cannot
climb out."

"We'll save you!" said Practical Pig
bravely.

The Three Little Pigs made a long,
strong rope from some vines.

"Catch this rope!" called
Practical Pig.

He let down one end of the rope
into the well.

Li'l Wolf grabbed it tightly.

But—oh, no!
SLIP...SLIP...SPLASH!!!

Practical Pig's feet slipped.
He fell into the well, too.

"Oh, dear!" cried the other pigs.
"Can you throw us the rope?"

"No," said Practical Pig. "The top of the well is too high. I cannot throw that far. Make another rope!"

"Oh, dear, oh, dear," cried the two little pigs. "We'll try."

They pulled and they pulled at another
vine.

Just then the Big Bad Wolf crept up behind
them.

Then he jumped at them.

"Aha!" cried the Big Bad Wolf. "Two
fat little pigs for Li'l Wolf and me!"

He popped both pigs into his sack.
One little pig said, "Wait, Mr. Wolf.
Li'l Wolf needs help. He fell into an old
well."

"Ha! You cannot fool me!" said the Big
Bad Wolf. "You want me to look down the well.
Then you will push me in."

The Big Bad Wolf closed the sack and
started home.

Then he heard Li'l Wolf's voice.

"It's true, Dad! I am stuck in the well with Practical Pig. He tried to save me."

"Oh, no!" cried the Big Bad Wolf. "How can I save you?"

The Big Bad Wolf looked worried.
"Ask the two little pigs,"
Li'l Wolf answered. "They will
help you."

The Big Bad Wolf let the two little pigs
out of the sack.

He really did not want to do that *at all.*

But he wanted to save his son.

The pigs quickly showed the Big Bad Wolf
how to make a vine rope.

"We'll let one end of the rope down and pull them up," the pigs said.

"I'll do it," said the Big Bad Wolf.

He pulled and he pulled.
Suddenly out they flew!
Li'l Wolf and Practical Pig were
glad to be saved.
"Hurray!" the other pigs cried.

The Big Bad Wolf kissed Li'l Wolf.

"Let's go home," the Big Bad Wolf said.

He wanted to take the juicy pigs home, too.

He was very hungry.

But he could not do that.

They had helped save Li'l Wolf.

"It is too bad we lost our baskets,"
said Practical Pig. "We could have a picnic."

"Baskets?" said the Big Bad Wolf. "Are these yours? I found them in the woods."

They all had lunch together.
And they all had a good time.
Even the Big Bad Wolf.
What a surprise that was to him!

The next day Li'l Wolf found a note
pinned to the wall.

"Read it to me, please," groaned
the Big Bad Wolf.

The note said:

"You are not such a big bad wolf after all! Signed, The Three Little Pigs"

"Oh, no!" cried the Big Bad Wolf. "Pigs are not supposed to like me!"

"Wait, Dad, I have a note too!" Li'l Wolf said.
He raced upstairs to his desk.

"Look, Dad!"

Li'l Wolf had pinned his gold star to another note:

Finally the Big Bad Wolf smiled.
He was really happy, after all!